SEASON ONE: EPISODE ONE

SUNSET CHRONICLES

LAST LIGHT

PAUL STEPHENSON

HOLLOW STONE

Contents

Note for readers

Last Light is the first episode of *The Sunset Chronicles*, a monthly sci-fi serial. Think of it like a series, much like you'd get on your favourite tv streaming service. There are seasons, split up into episodes (five per season). Each episode is designed to be read in roughly two hours, though fast readers may blast through them even quicker, and those who like to really get stuck into the story may take longer. They're intended to be thrilling and exciting, and are released regularly each month so that you can keep up with the story even if you have a hectic schedule. And who doesn't, these days? It's perfect for if you want to slip some space horror into your lunch break, or if you want to binge it of an evening.

Also, although *The Sunset Chronicles* is a story that stretches from the ice moon of Europa to every corner of the globe, its author remains English. As such, international readers should note that spellings are of the UK variation of English, so if you see a typo, it must be because of that.

If you're in the UK and you see a typo, it must be your imagination.

Prelude

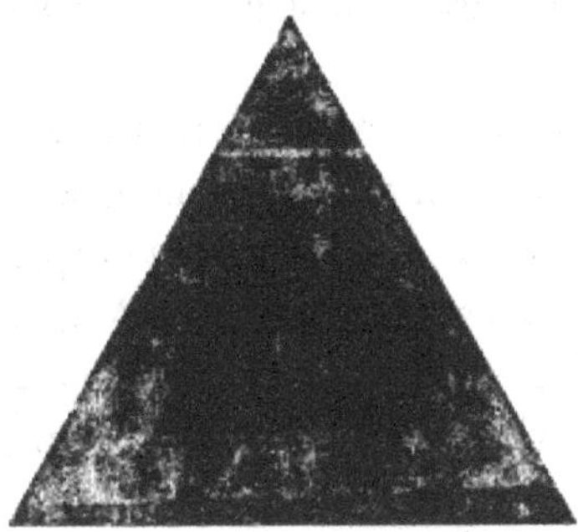

15th March, 2119. London, third protectorate of Sunset

Well, Jimmy, the world has gone to shit. Since there's nothing much better to do than sit around and wait for the whole bloody thing to come crashing down around our ears, I might as well write to you. Feels strange, taking to paper and ink. Who knows, perhaps this will be one of the last things ever written by man or beast on this stupid, petulant little rock of ours. The whole poxy enterprise, all up in smoke. It'd be funny, if I wasn't caught up in it.

As I speak the sky is red. Not one of those nice autumnal sunsets that has everyone reaching for their pads so they can layer a thousand mods to it and post it to their feed and wow a thousand strangers. Blood red. Everywhere. A world cast in shades of blood, day and night. Well, what's left of the days.

How the hell did we fuck everything up so badly, Jimmy?

Yellowstone. How many tonnes of toxic shit has it spilled into the atmosphere over the last few weeks? I saw on the feeds it's enough that even the poles have red skies. Just what we need after decades of the Mar, a fucking volcano killing the atmosphere.

Yesterday, a rain came down as thick and black as ink. Shit, if ever there was a metaphor. It stained the ground and tasted of old pennies.

As I write this, I'm watching the feeds, waiting for a man to announce to the world he killed millions of people. Shit, billions. With a smile on his face and a song in what passes for his heart. There's going to be a war. More will die. Maybe everyone.

We tried to stop this, but the more you look at it, the harder it gets to work out what path led us here, let alone who can lead us out of it. Did we do this to ourselves? I look back on the last nine years and I can't even fathom where the truth lies anymore.

Then there's the teeps. Fuck, the teeps. What a fucking mess.

I never thought I'd come to be glad you're not here with me, old friend. But that's where we are. Wherever we're heading, we're going to wish we were already dead.

I guess I'll see you soon, old friend.

Roman.

Chapter One

ISS Minos, en-route to the ice moon of Europa. Mission day 1597, Earth year 2107

Stretching her legs out, Wyn kicked off the soft rubber pumps designed to hug the floor in zero-g and let her feet breathe on the dash, the pale pink of her soles in stark contrast to the darkness of her skin and the sky beyond. She had the flight module to herself tonight, as most nights.

Night. What a concept.

The view from the cockpit remained the same. Endless black, perforated by pricks of light. Nudging the pad near her foot from its cradle, it floated up and across. Grabbing it, she flicked through the screens, calling up the music player. Sam Cooke. A change is gonna come.

She damn well hoped so.

Clicking play, the music swelled as well as it could through the battered speaker Wyn had hooked up. She sighed, thinking of the pictures of Sam Cooke on the back of her Baba's old records.

'Good evening, Commander,' a voice said, mechanised and slightly slurred.

'Miles, my good man,' Wyn said, leaning back in her chair. 'How are you on this fine evening?'

'I am well, Commander. My operational efficiency has increased by a standard one point seven percent through judicious rerouting of my subroutines.'

He sounded pleased, as Wyn guessed he had every right to be. A series of disasters saw sentient AI outlawed back on earth, but Miles was the pet project of the ISS Minos's chief systems engineer, Hamza. He represented the cutting edge in AI tech, even if he did sound like a drunk Etonian most of the time.

'Well,' she said, smiling, 'every boy needs a hobby.' She rubbed her eyes. She should go to bed. 'What can I do for you, anyway?'

'Captain Davis has requested a briefing with on-shift crew in the mess at twenty-two-hundred. I know you're not technically on shift, but I thought you'd like to know.'

Wyn glanced at her pad, and saw the alert come through. 'So he has, thanks buddy.' She popped open a blister-packed snack, letting the tasteless nugget of bug-based protein float up to her mouth.

Even through the munching of the snack and the music, she could tell Miles had more to add. 'Anything else?'

'Are you still having trouble sleeping, Commander?'

'Night's still young, Miles.'

'I checked the rota. It's your rotation for a sleep shift this evening.'

She sighed, rolling her eyes at the empty seat. 'Have you been letting Ermine get to you about my sleeping habits again, Miles?' Her poor excuse for an XO was far too interested in her sleeping patterns. Four years in, she was still listening to his gripes. Wyn didn't need much sleep. Never had. Didn't much see what the fuss was. 'Do we need to have a conversation about you being an old maid again?'

'I'd remind you, Commander, that I'm incorporeal, and therefore incapable of fulfilling the roles and responsibilities of a maid. But I would remind you that we're coming up to what Captain Davis calls 'the business end' of the mission, and he and the rest of the crew are relying...'

'Fine,' Wyn replied, holding her hands up. 'I'll go to bed. To get you off my back. I came in here because I thought looking at the stars for a bit might help relax me, but that's clearly not going to work with you buzzing in my ears,' she lied.

'I didn't mean...'

'I know,' Wyn sighed. Damn, but she did feel tired. And guilty. 'Come on, Miles, Don't be a buzzkill. Come and listen to records with me.'

'Records?'

'Fine, songs. Whatever. Don't be a pedant. Let me tell you about this song and why it's so great.'

'Commander, we've had this conversation on no less than twenty-seven separate occasions over the course of this mission. I lack the cognitive pathways required to appreciate the distinction and benefit between separate musical compositions, or the capacity to enjoy it.'

'You know,' Wyn replied, leaning forward to the pad and skimming through the fresh set of computational data for their approach vector, 'if you do want to become an evolved being, you're going to have to wrap your circuits around the concept of art at some point.'

Staring out of the thick glass, she located Jupiter, still a distant spectre, hanging low in the sky to their port side. Exactly where it should be.

'I am perfectly capable of understanding the basic concepts of art, and literature, and humour. It's just...'

He paused.

'Just what?'

'I fail to see the comfort in it that you humans do. I'm also not convinced it's a natural by-product of intelligence. There are a number of sea mammals on Earth who possess levels of intelligence, broadly speaking, in line with your own. And they do not create art.'

'That's why they never made it out of the sea,' she said, sighing. 'You know what?'

'You're too tired for this conversation?'

'Am I ever not?' She stood, clicking over the pad to autopilot. 'Good night, Commander.'

'Keep an eye on my calculations for me?'

'Of course.'

She was tired. That much was true. But she'd been tired for the best part of four years, unable to remember the last time she'd managed a night of uninterrupted sleep.

This was hardly her first time riding the vastness of space, but nothing could have prepared her for this mission. Short runs ferrying yuppies to the moon and parts to the International Space Station for the Juno mission were not the same thing as four years headed away from home.

No matter what the job, she'd always had the option of looking in the rear-view and seeing home, somewhere out there. Not anymore. Ever since the Minos had reached the point where the blue speck was no longer visible to the naked eye, sleep had completely eluded her.

She wasn't alone. Most of the crew had struggled within a few weeks of leaving Earth behind as they hurtled through the vastness of space at mind-scrambling speed, pushing well beyond the limits of anything humans had achieved before. As the mission pilot, Wyn herself was the proud owner of several records. Furthest flight from Earth. Longest stint for a single pilot. Fastest pilot ever.

As she left the cockpit she took one last look at the stars and tried to remind herself why she was here.

Earth—that little blue dot too far away to see—was dying, and they were going to save it. A pretty grandiose aim for a little Nigerian English girl, and worth inconveniencing herself over. Even if it would be the best part of a decade before she'd be back on that dot.

The prime of her life. She could be settling down; taking a cushy low-risk high-orbit route, flying businessmen from the east to the west, staying in swanky hotels. Find some hunky co-pilot. Maybe one who looked like those pictures of Sam Cooke on the back of her Baba's records.

Or she could be back with her Baba on his farm, getting in trouble with the local cops. Or the local boys. Not crawling endlessly through a tin can hundreds of thousands of miles from home with a computer who didn't like music as the closest thing she had to a best friend.

Floating through to the bunks, she climbed into her rack, pulling the curtain closed without bothering to get undressed first. Weariness crept over her, and her eyes closed against the darkness.

Images of home danced through her subconscious as she drifted toward sleep. London, the place she still thought of as home, as they'd left it. Jumbled images of her mother crying, clinging to Wyn, waiting for the rescue boat. The glide, as they viewed the desolation. Back to before the waves, her brother's hand in her own, standing in the doorway of their home. To looking out one the side of the boat after the water, staring into murky brown water. The smell. The anxious faces. The desperate tears.

The wall of water.

She awoke with a start, head bumping on the bunk above. Sweat soaked her clothes.

Grasping for the porthole, she pulled up the flimsy plastic screen to reveal the view to the stars beyond. Groggily, she tried to centre herself by working out their position from the stars. Craning round, she could make out Jupiter, hanging heavy in space. Unmoving, despite the pace at which the Minos hurtled toward it.

'Miles,' she said, voice cracking. She licked her lips to try and get some moisture going. She needed something to drink which wasn't coffee, though coffee would do at a stretch.

'Yes, Commander?'

'What time is it?'

'You are still on sleep rotation. You should try and return to your sleep state, although I can sense you have an elevated heart...'

'What time is it, Miles?'

'Twenty-three hundred.'

'Is the briefing still on?'

'It hasn't started yet, there was a delay.'

She swung her feet out of the bunk, whipped off her sodden top and threw it down to the far end of the bunk, reaching for another from the rack behind her. She'd definitely need a shower at some point.

The Minos might be the largest vehicle ever constructed, but it would be pushing it to say it was roomy. Essentially a giant missile, she had four separate sections, three of which were open to the crew. There was the tiny flight deck, which housed a maximum of two, and the crew deck. This long tube held separate rooms for the mess, workplaces for the science team, a medical facility which made the flight deck look roomy, the Captain's office, and the bunks. This section had two thin corridors connected to giant thrusters either side of the ship. Beyond this, a gigantic cargo bay housed the mission equipment—the lander, mining equipment, and everything else. Beyond again were the main thrusters, which burned at a steady rate to hurtle them at Jupiter at a speed which made Wyn's head hurt to think about.

Even at her height—she was the crew's shortest member—she had to stoop to get through the doorways in and out of the bunks. Passing empty workspaces, she got to the mess—a self-contained room doubling as the sole space big enough to give briefings. She floated through the corridor, grabbed the door, and peered through the hatch. The whole of the rest of the crew watched, even those who should have been on sleep shift. Captain Davis addressed them, waving around his no-spill mug as he spoke.

She turned the hatch. The Captain stopped, and everyone turned to stare. Ermine, the XO, checked his watch.

'Sorry,' she muttered, taking the final empty chair in the starkly lit room.

Captain Davis gave her a warm smile and continued. 'We're coming to it. Any complacency that's been creeping into our work, myself included, over the last few weeks and months, it stops. Run your drills like it's the first day. We're prepared, but we need to sharpen our minds out of the stagnation from being out here for four years. Get sharp. Get focused. Make sure you're sleeping. Stay hydrated. Double check your routines, triple check them. If you need help, ask for it. The seven of you represent the best and brightest Earth has to offer, but they designed mission with single specialists, so if you fail at your mission nobody else is going to notice until it's too late. If you can't do it, chances are nobody else can. Let's tighten everything up before we make that final push, yeah?'

Faces nodded around the table, and a few smirks exchanged.

'Uh,' Barnes said, raising his hand like he was in class. 'I'd like some help, please?'

Captain Davis sighed, sitting down and taking a sip from his cup. He shrugged and gestured to the Doctor the floor was his.

'It's an issue with the working conditions,' Barnes said, furrowing his brow. 'You see, Hamza is at the next desk across from me, and he keeps farting. I've got to say, I'm worried he might have access to some food source the rest of us don't have, because it smells like something died.'

Hamza picked up a morsel of food from his plate and threw it at the doctor, smirking. It arced lazily across to him.

The doctor caught it with his mouth. 'I'm serious,' he continued, chewing. 'You know, I don't enjoy having to examine the crew's stools at the best of times, but he let one drop yesterday that made me think they'd come to life and were planning a mutiny.'

'Okay,' Captain Davis said, holding his hands up, ignoring the sniggers around the table. 'Let's get to it. One week until we get to Europa. The time for fucking around is over, okay?'

Barnes held his hands up in acquiescence and stood, smirking at Hamza, who made mock threatening gestures back across the table. The rest of the crew rose from their seats, the low buzz of conversation and laughter taking over the silence.

'Wyn,' the Captain said, his deep voice cutting through the noise even at a hush. 'A word?'

'Sure,' she replied, getting back into the chair she was only half out of.

Zoe, ship's biologist and mission specialist, gave Wyn a smile of solidarity. Stef, one of the two engineers, arched her eyebrow. The ship's XO, Ermine, was last to leave, hanging around long enough to hear what was being said until he realised Captain Davis wouldn't start talking until he left. He got the hint eventually, pulling the hatch closed behind him. If Wyn opened it quick enough, he'd probably tumble back through it with a cup to his ear.

'So,' the Captain said, 'how's our course looking?'

Wyn shrugged. 'Within mission parameters, Captain.' This was, of course, an understatement. She might have been out of the cockpit for a few hours, but she could give a cast iron guarantee they'd be over ninety-nine point nine recurring percent accurate to their plotted trajectory. In other words, the distance from the flight plan wouldn't be more than the width of an A4 paper. If that.

The Captain nodded, and took a sip from his coffee. 'And you?'

'Fine.'

'Still not sleeping?'

'Are you?'

Davis sighed. 'Come on, Commander, give me a break. I'm not trying to attack you here.'

'No, Captain,' she said. 'I'm not sleeping well. And before you say anything, I don't want to see Barnes about a sedative. You know as well as I do they don't provide restful sleep, and they dull the reflexes far beyond operational safety levels. I don't think anyone wants that.'

'Nobody wants you so tired you steer us into a gas giant, either,' the Captain replied. There was no malice or anger in his voice, but a quiet authority which reminded Wyn of sitting across from her Baba, getting told off for skipping school.

'I'm fine,' Wyn stressed, taking his hand, the contrast of her dark skin against his made starker after four years with no sunlight.

'If you say so,' he said, patting her hand as he pulled his own away. 'But you are still on sleep shift for a few hours yet. Go to bed, that's an order.'

'Sure,' she said, pushing her chair back and getting to her feet.

The Captain looked so tired, sat at the table, nursing his cup anxiously.

'You know,' she said, 'I could say the same to you. Who's telling you to go to bed?'

He chuckled. 'You know full well the XO is on my back almost as much as he's on yours.'

'I doubt it,' she muttered, turning to the door, but he either didn't hear or elected to ignore it.

Outside, the crew busied themselves, the majority on a day cycle in opposition to her own. Not that day and night meant anything out here, but the ship's computer at least tried to give them some semblance of normality to their routines. Wyn's pod would be darker than Li Wei's, or Zoe's, the systems trying to convey a sense of night to her as though the last four years had been anything else.

The bunks were at the end of the corridor. She should head back to her rack, at least attempt to get a few more hours of sleep. There was a busy day of computations and course trajectory mathematics to get through. Mission control had put a request through for numbers on a new scenario that would save them a few days. Wyn knew there was no way they'd work, but she'd have to hold their hands all the way through before they'd agree with her.

Go to bed.

Her eyes felt heavy. She sat at one of the empty desks, Hamza having turned in right after the meeting. Her eyes closed.

A busy street. People rushed about. She stood in the doorway, laughing at them. Her brother splashed in puddles on the doorstep, his wellies covered in cartoon dinosaurs. He slipped his hand in hers.

Her eyes snapped open, and she sat up with a start.

Her breath slowly came back to normal. She watched the corridor. Nobody had seen.

'Hey, Zo,' she called out, as the scientist headed past, clipboard in hand.

Zoe turned, giving Wyn a warm smile. 'Hey, stranger.'

'Want to hang out?'

Chapter Two

Tijuana, Mexico

With the sun beating down on the ground, reflecting off the gleaming metal and glass of downtown Tijuana, Lois's pale skin sizzled under layers of sun cream and a wide-brimmed hat. She'd bought it to protect herself from burning, but there was no protection from the heat. She wasn't quite old enough to be getting hot flushes, but who'd notice them in this weather, anyway?

Her business suit wasn't helping much, either. Beige was a bad choice, sweat patches soaking through the armpits of her woollen jacket from the shirt underneath. Her face was sweaty, too, lending enough humidity to turn her hair into a bird's nest.

Still, if this went well, she'd be back in the States by the evening. Twenty miles away a glide waited, ready to take her back to her girls. Just the small matter of confronting a billionaire property magnate with his laundry list of crimes and getting him to surrender himself to the authorities to get through before that.

Walking through the doors of Coyne Enterprises, the blast of cool air setting her teeth on edge, instantly cooling the sweat running down her temple. That coupled with the mound of fresh apples freely available on the central desk of the foyer screamed of Felipe Coyne's ostentatiousness. A block away, his properties housed thousands in tightly packed hell-holes not fit for human habitation, their inhabitants largely on the brink of starvation—while here he paid stupid amounts on air conditioning and fruit that was harder to come by than gold. It took every fibre of her being not to grab one of the shiny red orbs as she walked past.

'Ms Pertin,' an officious little man said as she approached the security barriers. His eyes swept over her with no small manner of disgust, which would have pissed her off if she hadn't experienced it every day for the last two months.

'Javier,' she replied, striding through the barriers with as much purpose as she could muster. In truth, her heart rate was already elevated slightly, the anticipation of what she was about to do tingling at the ends of her fingers. She wished she could have brought a weapon in—hell, a whole team to back her up—but here she was, alone and about to confront a man implicated in countless murders to cover up his crimes, in his own fortress. She couldn't even wear an Oc to let Findlay, her handler, know what was going on, since Coyne was paranoid as hell about, well, exactly what was about to happen to him, in fairness.

Lining up for an elevator, she checked herself in one of the wide mirrors. She looked like absolute shit. Her blonde hair had absorbed all the moisture dripping off her skin and turned to a ball of yarn, her makeup testing the limits of its water resistance just beyond breaking point. She looked all of her forty-seven years, the lines of worry causing her eyes to look like deep craters.

Mental note—don't wear flannel suits ever again.

The doors opened, and she stepped in.

Checking the readout on her wrist, she was about fifteen minutes early to meet Coyne. Her finger ran down the front seam of her jacket, feeling for the tiny ridge where the bug sat affixed to listen to every word said in this meeting. A damn shame she couldn't transmit, but those were the cards she had.

After seventeen floors, the doors slid back open, revealing yet another foyer, and the smiling figure of Coyne. He stood waiting, a wide smile across his face, his hands outstretched.

'Lois,' he said, nary a trace of his Mexican accent remaining.

Stepping out into the foyer, she realised her mistake too late. From each side, guards stepped forward, grabbing her by the upper arms. Whipping her head round to look at her attackers, she was met with the butt of a pistol descending, cracking her on the head.

Everything blurred, swirled.

She dropped to her knees, but never made the floor, her weight taken by the hefty guards, pulling her forward.

'I...' she protested, groggily.

Her shoes dragged across the floor, as she struggled to catch her bearings. The ringing that sounded like an alarm faded away, and her vision came back into focus. The thought of struggling came to mind, but she couldn't feel her feet, so she let the burly men drag her into Coyne's office, where they unceremoniously dumped her onto a sofa.

Coyne took a seat at his desk, surprising in its lack of ostentatiousness. 'Lois, my dear, I can't tell you how disappointed I am,' he said, a chuckle dancing at the edge of his voice. He sure as hell didn't sound disappointed.

Lois said nothing, mainly because she wasn't yet sure she could talk. The two guards stood either side of her as she swayed back and forth on a linen sofa as drab as everything else in the room.

Coyne motioned to the guards, they skulked silently away to the door, pulling it closed behind them. Lois had no doubt they'd be staying close by in case she tried something.

Groggily, she tried to compose a plan, The options were fairly limited. Play dumb? She was here to confront him anyway, so there didn't seem much point in playing dumb. A pistol whip to the head didn't change much.

Coyne reached into his desk and pulled out a pistol, an elaborate gold number which stood out in stark contrast to the rest of his office.

Okay, that changed things a little.

'Is it too late to say you're under arrest?' Lois asked, voice catching in her throat. Reaching up to her head, she touched the part throbbing with a dull ache. It was already swelling up.

Coyne barked a hollow laugh. 'Lois, did you not think I knew you were an Interpol agent from the first day you came here?'

She gave her own hollow laugh in return, trying desperately to ignore the flash of light reflecting off the golden gun. Every part of her screamed to turn and run, to beg, to plead for her life. But that would be a mistake. She straightened her back and fixed him with a glare and a smile. 'Actually, I know you didn't. But I'm curious to know how you found out. If you knew I was an agent and you still showed me everything you've showed me in the last few weeks, then you are a stone cold idiot. You realise I've sent that back already to HQ, right? We've logged enough evidence against you and your company to have you inside a cell for the next few decades.'

A twitch around the eyes. That was all it took to let Lois know she had him. She smiled, heart pounding in her chest and head throbbing with pain, trying desperately not to show either.

'You're bluffing,' Coyne said.

'I don't need to bluff,' Lois said. 'I have proof. Which one of your goons took my bag?'

Coyne leaned forward and tapped a button. No sound omitted from it, but a second later one of the guards came back through the door and handed Coyne Lois's bag.

'Go ahead, look inside,' Lois said. 'There's a pad in there.'

The pad was a standard issue Interpol warrant. All it needed was Coyne's DNA, which he helpfully provided the moment he lifted the pad out. The screen came on, and Coyne's face drained to grey as he saw the crest of the Interpol warrant flash up on the screen. Already, Interpol's servers would be recording that he'd seen the warrant, as it began to scrawl through the array of charges being considered against him.

Key word being 'considered'.

'So,' Lois said, getting up from the sofa on shaky legs.

The goon looked at his boss for guidance. He got none, Coyne's gaze stuck on the thorough list of his transgressions.

'Now you know I'm on the level,' Lois said, 'I imagine you're working out the cost of killing me.' She perched on the edge of his desk, mostly because her legs remained unsteady. Her stomach churned, and she wondered if she might have a touch of concussion. Just get through the next ten minutes, and she could be back out in the baking heat, heading to a glide, and away from having to appear like the tough Interpol agent she never quite felt up to being.

'You bitch,' Coyne said.

'Settle down, Felipe,' she replied, heart hammering in her mouth. This was an act she put on, this bravura, and she was never particularly impressed by the performance. It seemed to be working on Coyne, however. For now. 'I'm not here to cart you off to jail, much as it would give me endless pleasure to do so. We know you have lawyers who could tie us up in court for the next ten years, if you chose to go down that route. In the meantime, that's ten more years of your tenants living in slums I wouldn't let a rat sleep in. We're willing to offer a compromise. You're going to clean up your act, Felipe. A lengthy trial, that's got to cost you, what, a couple of million credits? Not to mention the stain on what you laughingly call a reputation.'

'What do you want me to do?' Coyne asked, his voice hovering somewhere between disdain and begging. 'Hand out apples to everyone in the barrio?'

She leaned in so her breath gently moved the whiskers adorning his top lip. 'If you really think the only option to make the lives of your people better is to give them apples, you're even more of a craven excuse for a human being than I thought you were.'

She pulled back, getting back off the table, taking her bag but leaving the pad with him. It had, after all, done its job.

'So what?' Coyne asked, any trace of humour absent from the words.

'You have six months to get your house in order. All your accommodation—and I do mean all of it, even those you sub-let—must be fully code compliant within the next six months. We will be inspecting. I don't care what it costs, Coyne, it'll be a drop in the ocean compared to what you'd face if we take action against you. Make no mistake, you fail to right the wrongs you see listed on that pad, we'll take you into custody. Speak to your lawyers. Whatever you want. They'll tell you it's a hell of a lot cheaper this way. Hell, you can even get some good PR out of it, make the run for the legislature you've always talked about. It's entirely up to you.'

She stood, heading to the door to find it blocked by the burly security guard. He looked caught between his desire to avoid jail and to slam the butt of his pistol into her head again.

'If you're wondering the best way to apologise for your actions and avoid being arrested for assaulting an Interpol agent, I'd suggest getting out of my way.'

The guard looked over Lois's shoulder. Lois resisted the urge to look back to see Coyne's face, waiting for him to release her.

Instead, the cock of the hammer of the gold gun sounded, and the guard's hand shot out, clamping around Lois's neck and lifting her so her toes brushed madly against the floor. Fighting for breath, she scrabbled madly at the arm holding her, scratching at the skin with her nails, breaking the skin and drawing blood to no avail. The cold gold muzzle of the gun pressed to the base of her skull stopped all that. She went still, staring into the eyes of the guard, a blank dead stare looking through her to his boss.

Coyne leaned in until it was his hot breath on the back of her neck.

'You must think I'm a fucking idiot if you think that kind of scare tactic is going to work on me,' he whispered. 'This is my town, and nothing happens here I don't want.'

The guard released her, and this time there was nobody to stop her crashing to the floor, knees banging into hard marble in a fresh burst of pain. She desperately tried to take air in, breaths coming in ragged bursts.

Looking up, Coyne towered over her. He raised the gun. Smirking, he blew her a kiss. 'Say goodnight, agent.'

Chapter Three

The Key, Minor Moon Station

'I dream of victory,' the old man said, his voice little more than a whisper. Strands of grey hair clung to the skin stretched thin over his skull, mottled with brown spots. His face was kindly enough, but so damned old. Judd couldn't imagine himself wanting to live as long as this guy.

Judd caught a reflection of himself—doughy, skin pasty and grey, face covered in days-old stubble, dark hair in need of a wash—wheeling an old man about in a wheelchair. Who was he kidding? There was no way he'd last as long as this old fart.

Still, there the old fart was, one-hundred-and-twenty-eight years old, staring back down at the Earth from the Moon. Sure, he'd docked at the lowest budget moon base, where you kind of had to crane your neck a bit to get a decent view of the blue marble, but as Judd pushed him up to the viewing port, his face lit up with the same mix of awe and vague disappointment Judd saw every day.

The Key might be low class, but it wasn't cheap. As a result, most of its clientele were like Mr Walker here, those who spent more than they could afford to get there. Old people, mostly, those for whom the lustre of space travel had a nostalgic tinge, laced with stories of Aldrin and Armstrong. They'd saved up all their lives, now they were going to blow it on a trip to the moon to stay at a place with the feel of a cheap motel. And why not? They'd earned it, no point handing it down to greedy next generations. Then they got here to a grimy spacedock lit by cheap neon lights and as they looked back at that little blue marble their first thought was always whether it had been worth the effort.

Judd could sympathise. He was only in his twenties, but every time he looked out of that window, he wondered how he'd ended up here.

'Victory?' he asked the old man.

'Hmmm?'

The old man stared back at the Earth, clearing his throat with a rattle which made Judd wonder if he'd have to call the emergency crews. He sure as shit wouldn't be giving mouth-to-mouth.

'Oh, yes,' Mr Walker replied, dabbing away whatever leakage had emanated from his wrinkled mouth with a handkerchief that might predate its owner. Judd couldn't place the accent. 'Victory. Odd, after all this time. Grudges you hold. I once bet a man a princely sum I would beat him to seeing this view.' He coughed again, the one tumbling into many. Dry, heaving coughs echoed through the corridor.

Judd put his hand out to steady him, not wanting to touch him, but not wanting him to pitch forward onto the cold tiles, either. Jesus, was he about to have his first actual death? 'Did you beat him?' he asked, as much to take the old man's mind off the coughs as to get an answer.

'I should say so,' he wheezed. 'He died decades ago.' Another sound, which Judd thought might be the start of another round of coughs but turned out to be a hollow laugh. 'Strange,' the old man continued, looking out at the stars. 'All this time later I don't much feel like I won.'

'He was your friend?'

'Something like that.'

Judd nodded. He didn't care, one way or the other. His job was to make sure the old duffer had a decent time up here on the Key, spend time with him, give him a dinner, stick him on a shuttle home, pick up another old duffer, and do the same with them.

These were the ones who paid for the 'personal services' tours. When he'd first turned up for the job, the other new arrivals giggled and jeered at him for getting saddled with the 'personal services' gig, but he'd been pleased. He'd thought he'd be knee deep in middle aged divorcees burning through their husband's money, wanting to join the twenty-thousand-mile-high club, but no such luck. Otherwise he might have earned enough money to get off this shit pit, onto a proper gig.

Still, it could be worse, he thought, as he looked down on the old man's sallow skin and liver spots. Imagine having to play nurse to this old fucker. Probably shits nothing but brown water.

'So,' Judd said, clapping his hands together, making his first attempt to move the guy to the next part of the tour. 'There she is.' He knew full well it'd take another three or four goes to move him on. It always did. But you had to make the first one before you could make the second, and so on. This was the only bit of the tour anyone cared about, but if they didn't keep the traffic moving nobody would get to see it, and everyone would start demanding refunds. There was nothing the top brass at The Key liked less than refunds.

'Beautiful,' the old man said. 'What's left of her, at any rate.'

'You must have seen some things over the years, eh?'

'There wasn't so much blue when I grew up.'

Sure, Judd thought. And whose generation do we have to thank for that?

'I bet,' he replied. He wasn't there to get angry with the old people who'd sold his generation and those before down the river. If he did, he'd never get through the tours.

'Forgive me. You must get nothing but old bastards up here reminiscing about their sad old lives,' the old man said, turning to Judd with a wicked smile.

Judd couldn't help but let out a chuckle. He looked around to check there were no bosses around. 'None quite at your vintage though, sir.'

'Yeah, well, nobody asks to live this long, kid. I don't recommend it, either.' He craned round to look behind Judd. Judd followed his gaze to a bunch of other seniors crowding around the larger second window, no doubt wondering why they didn't stump up the cash for the personal services package.

Mr Walker gave a hollow laugh. 'You probably look down there and see a bunch of old farts. I look down there and see a bunch of punk kids.'

'What about me?'

'You might as well be a foetus.'

'Well, Mr Walker. If you've seen enough of the view, perhaps you'll allow this foetus the pleasure of your company for dinner? I believe we're serving Beef Wellington this evening.'

'Bullshit,' Walker laughed. 'You're serving bugs, crushed up and blended and mushed into a paste and given the flavour of Beef Wellington. I didn't pay anywhere near enough to be getting the real deal. You forget, kid, I grew up before the Mar, back when food was food. I remember what a good Beef Wellington tastes like.'

'I can assure you our expert chefs...'

'Don't bullshit a bullshitter, kid.' He waved his hand. 'It's okay, I know you're doing your job. Let's go eat some bugs.'

The dining hall had two sections—one for the higher paying customers where they could eat on private tables with their handlers, one where the rest of the masses had to settle for long tables where they looked like prisoners, or pigs at a trough. The latter group couldn't come in until the high rollers had already gotten their food, which meant handlers like Judd sometimes had to conduct some pretty delicate negotiations to get their people into the room. Some came back to the Key a few times—they never came back on the cheap ticket. Since the high rollers had held them up on their first visit, they made sure to inflict the same misery on the next round of cheapskates. That this happened every damn time told Judd everything he needed to know about humanity in the twenty-second century.

Thankfully, Walker didn't bust his ass too much, and they'd gotten here early. Judd wheeled Mr Walker to a table and went to fetch their meals.

If there was one thing he could count on his clients to do, it was to bitch about the food. It pissed Judd off. There was barely any so-called 'real' food back on Earth, so how the hell they expected to get fresh meat and veg out here on this rock was beyond Judd.

Judd was of the first generation raised knowing nothing but reclaimed carbon. Sure, he'd occasionally had meat and veg as a kid, but what kid got excited about real vegetables, anyway? By the time he was old enough to care much about food, he was already used to the carbon.

He never saw what the fuss was, either. It tasted fine. Some of it was even pretty good. The problem was people's hang-ups about where it came from, and because they kept trying to make it into the food they couldn't have anymore.

The server handed over two lumps of steaming slop, a perfect example of how not to present reclaimed carbon. Judd had no idea what a Beef Wellington should look like, smell like, or taste like, but he was pretty sure it wasn't anything like what he had to carry back to Mr Walker. In fact, there wasn't a reclaimator in existence could take processed bug carcasses and make it taste like what this old man wanted. So why bother? If they gave Judd control of the kitchen, he could whip them up some harissa patties that tasted divine.

Mr Walker turned his nose up at the plate as Judd placed it in front of him, but picked his fork up to eat. At least he could do that. Judd had been lucky so far—two years in the job and he'd not had to feed anyone yet, let alone do anything worse.

'So,' Judd said, picking up his own fork. 'What did you do, Mr Walker?'

'Oh, I'm sure you're not interested in that. I'm more interested in you. How does a guy end up in a place like this? Pretty far from home, I imagine?'

Judd shrugged. He wasn't used to his clients asking him personal questions, and sure as shit wasn't about to tell the old man the truth. 'Kind of fell into it. I always liked the idea of the moon stations growing up. Kind of like the old Wild West.'

'You wanted to be a cowboy?'

Judd laughed. 'Something like that. I dunno. I never found anything to fit before. I'm not so sure this does, either, but it pays the bills. Plus, the view's pretty good. And I get to meet some interesting people.'

'Oh, yeah?'

'Sure.'

They ate in silence for a moment, until Judd remembered he wasn't supposed to let the conversation die out.

'So, you remember the twentieth century?' he asked.

Walker chewed his food with a grimace, washing it down with some complimentary champagne. Judd was impressed the old fart could manage booze.

'Sure,' he said, finally. 'Onto my third century. Not a bad innings.'

'Any advice for a young man?'

'Don't trust anyone.'

Judd laughed. 'That's a little darker than I'd hoped.'

'Well, you asked.'

Judd nodded, chewing a mouthful of fake mashed potatoes. He looked at the old man. Not bad company. Better conversationalist than most of his clients. He liked days like today. Sometimes this job didn't even feel too much like a job. 'So what was it like?'

'What was what like?'

'The twentieth century.'

'I don't know. Looking back, it was a pretty good time, the last few years of it, anyway. An innocent time. It was after the turn of the century things pretty quickly started to go to shit. But if you'd have asked people back then, they would have laughed at the idea like it was some kind of golden age. Things got worse. Sometimes slowly, sometimes in a hurry. I remember my elders at the time telling me how much better it had been when they were young. The only reasonable conclusion is that things are on an eternal decline.'

'That's a cheery thought.'

He smiled, that wicked grin lighting up his eyes. 'Sorry, kid.'

They returned to silence for a moment, Judd trying to process what the old man had said. All those history lessons Judd had sat through in school—across from him was someone who'd lived through so much of it. He'd never thought about these old duffers like that.

Judd was so lost in thought he reached the end of his meal without realising it. He looked across at the old man, who sat grinning back at him.

'What?'

'You realise we never said a word to each other, right?'

The old man's mouth never moved as he said it.

Judd's blood ran cold, goose bumps popping out on his arms like a chill wind had blown through. Instinctively, he looked to the exits. No police, no fucking stormtroopers about to burst in. All was normal.

'Relax, kid,' the old man said, inside Judd's head. 'I'm not here to hurt you. I'm not here for anything to do with you. But it's nice to meet you.'

Judd tried to form a thought in his head to send back but couldn't. He'd never had a conversation with another teep before. He didn't even know how. He couldn't even say how he'd managed to speak to Walker a moment earlier.

'I'm...' Judd said, out loud, but there weren't words to follow it. His hackles were up. He wanted to run, to sprint for the exits. Take the first shuttle back.

'Don't worry about it, kid,' Walker said, out loud. He gave Judd a half smile. 'But what do you say you let me buy you a drink?'

Chapter Four

'Shouldn't you be sleeping?' Zoe asked, as Wyn sank into the science officer's comfortable chair.

'Can't,' Wyn huffed, picking up an old-fashioned paper text-book on Zoe's desk and flipping through it, eyes skimming over the formulas and notations. Same language as her own notepads, yet a completely different one.

'I can't wait to get to bed,' Zoe replied, dropping her pad onto the desk and rubbing her temples. 'I've spent the best part of seven hours looking at gene sequencing data which doesn't make sense. It's making my head go kerfluey.'

Wyn nodded, without the faintest idea what Zoe was on about. The science officer had tried to explain the basics to Wyn at least a dozen times over the past few years, but somehow the salient points never stuck. Besides, she had enough on her plate trying to keep the physics needed to plot their journey in her head; she didn't want to get it mixed up with organic chemistry and viral strains.

What little she did know would barely fill a Wikipedia entry. Twenty years ago, a blight had struck the crops of farms in South America, spreading its way across the world over the course of two years until over ninety percent of the world's farming stock disappeared. Arable, meat, and dairy—all hit. This blight became known as The Mar. Species numbers across the board began to tumble, and the petty animi of the world seemed to fall into insignificance for a few years. Of course, it didn't last long, and soon everyone went back to warring over what remained.

A decade or so later, a probe to one of Jupiter's moons sent back news—it had found an organic substance on the icy surface. Life. Once the news feeds had gone through their cycles of losing their collective shit over the discovery, they realised it wasn't as sexy a story as food riots and tsunamis.

Wyn didn't pay attention, to begin with. She'd seen algae growing on the International Space Station. Hell, she'd had to go and scrape that shit off on her first ever spacewalk. That wasn't much fun, given the amount of debris floating around up there. In fact, the continued resilience of that rusting old bucket of a space station was more of a mystery to her than whether there was organic life out there. If someone could present her with a real-life, standing-up-and-walking-around alien, she'd get excited. Until then, she wasn't getting het up about what was most likely a fungus or algae.

Then some boffins, including the woman staring through a microscope in front of her, found a genetic correlation between the data coming from Europa's surface and the Mar. Cue the news feeds losing their shit again. It was this link Zoe had explained to Wyn a thousand times, but Wyn still couldn't wrap her head around it. It didn't matter. The long and short of it was she had to fly Zoe and the others out to the ice moon to see if they could find a cure. Then she'd take them home again. Not much more than a glorified taxi driver. Wyn was cool with that though, there was a lot less responsibility on her shoulders than Zoe's.

'Problem with the data?' Wyn asked.

Zoe frowned. 'Not exactly. I don't know. I've spent so long looking at it, none of it makes sense anymore. I want to get down there so I can test some of these theories, examine exactly what the probe's been sending us.' She sighed. 'I guess we'll know soon enough.' Looking up at Wyn, the frown intensified. 'That's if you're not too tired to get us there without crashing into Jupiter.'

'Jesus, Zoe, you too? Look, Jupiter's pretty big. I think I'll be able to spot if we start drifting too close, okay?'

'Knock knock,' a quiet voice said behind them. Li Wei, the Minos's mechanical engineer, stood sheepishly in the doorway.

'Hey, Li,' Wyn said. 'How's my ship doing?'

'Good,' Li said. 'Zoe, have you seen the most recent probe data?'

'Yeah,' Zoe replied, her Australian accent deepening with her frustration. 'Damn signal loss, or interference or something. Something in the magnetosphere corrupting the data. Nothing else makes sense.'

'That's what I thought,' Li said, the furrow of his brow matching Zoe's.

'Ugh,' Wyn said, getting out of the comfortable chair. 'Shop talk. I'll leave you to it.'

'Get some sleep,' Zoe called after her.

Wyn waved back dismissively, and moved through to the next pod, where Barnes fussed over Stef in his med bay.

'Stop moving,' he said, holding a needle over the mechanic's right arm.

'I am not moving,' she protested, despite the evidence to the contrary. 'This is ridiculous. I'm not going to get tetanus from a piece of metal engineered to be free of contaminants in a vacuum.'

'That was five years ago, Stef. Hold still, will you?' Barnes always spoke to his patients like he had a cigarette dangling from one corner of his mouth, even though he'd had to kick the habit to get this posting. Wyn wasn't sure why he'd volunteered—he hated every aspect of the trip to his core.

'Evening, you two,' Wyn said, placing her head through the open door.

'Wyn,' Stef said, 'be a darling and get this oaf off me.'

'No can do, Stef,' Wyn replied. 'I try never to get between a doctor and their victim.'

'Patient, we prefer to call them,' Barnes said, waving the needle an inch above the mechanic's skin.

'I'll be calling you something else if you stick me with that!'

'Stef, has anyone told you that you sound more German the crosser you get?' Wyn said.

'Nein,' Stef said, pulling her arm away from the doctor. 'Wenn dieser blödes arschloch mich nicht loslässt, werde ich ihm meine wahre deutsche wut zeigen.'

'Hey, speak English, please, or I'll give you a double dose.'

'Fick dich.'

'That I understood,' Barnes said, finally getting the needle into Stef's arm.

'Have fun, you two,' Wyn said, turning away.

'Not so fast yourself there, young lady,' Barnes said. 'I need to have a talk with you about your sleeping habits. I've got a nice cocktail here I can give you, let you get some sleep?'

'Looks like you have quite enough on your hands. Another time?' Before the doctor could protest, she whirled round and back out of the door, straight into Ermine.

'Woah,' she said, confronted by the size of her XO.

'You think this is funny?' he asked, his face as stern as ever.

The smile dropped right off Wyn's face. 'Not really?'

Ermine liked to use the advantage of his height to loom whenever he wanted to appear commanding, which was most of the time. Given Wyn was the shortest crewmember, he was able to do this effortlessly, with his Harvard rower physique and chiselled catalogue model looks. On a crew where everyone had spent four years settling into a countenance of general amiableness, he'd been the lone holdout. He glowered with disdain at everyone on the crew, and Wyn seemed to bear the brunt most of all.

'I hope I don't need to remind you,' he said, in a voice both weary and sneering. 'You hold the lives of all of us in your hands. If you fuck up, even a little bit, you'll kill us, and consign billions of people back on Earth to death.'

'That one's pretty well burned into my consciousness, thanks.' She moved to push past him, but he blocked her.

'You need to go to your bunk and get some sleep. Every time we get in this cycle, you get more and more tired, and you drop the ball. I have to step in, we lose you for a day while you get better, and we do it again. How many times have I ordered you to get a sedative? Ten? It's getting tired, if you'll excuse the pun.'

'It's not much fun for me, either,' Wyn replied, eyes on the floor.

'We're getting down to brass tacks. We can't afford to lose you.' He leaned in. 'Go to fucking sleep, okay? That's an order.'

He pulled away, the heat of his breath sending shivers of revulsion down her spine. He turned away and headed through to the pod where Stef and Barnes had stopped arguing long enough to watch the show.

'Just so you know,' she called to Ermine's retreating shoulders, 'reminding me of the colossal burden on my shoulders isn't exactly the relaxant you might think it is.'

He was gone.

She sighed. He might be the biggest prick Wyn had encountered since she'd stopped ferrying businessmen about for a living, but he was right. She needed sleep. She also needed to model the points of entry, slingshots, and everything else, one more time, but she couldn't manage any of that in this state.

Crossing to the other side of the ship, she started towards the bunk. She floated past Hamza's office and stuck her head in.

'Hey.'

'Shouldn't you be sleeping?' he asked, without looking up from soldering a circuit board.

'Jesus fucking Christ, Hamza, you too?'

He chuckled, looking up at her.

'Shit,' Wyn said. 'Sorry.'

'Not my deity,' he shrugged.

'What you up to?'

'Upgrade to Miles's mainframe. That's why he's been quiet the last few hours.'

'Right,' she said. She hadn't noticed. She looked around Hamza's pod. The sole bona fide religious person on the crew, or at least the only one who prayed openly; his prayer mat sat rolled up on top of his cabinet. 'Hey, Hamz, I've been meaning to ask. Do you still try and face west when you pray? How do you work the direction out?'

'Hmmm? Oh, well, it's not a question of facing west, it's facing Mecca. So, I face the back of the ship. Figure that's the general direction.'

'Huh.'

He looked up and smiled. 'Wyn, I love you, but go to sodding bed, will you?'

She threw up her hands. 'Fine.' Turning away, she found herself face-to-face with the bunks. There was nobody else to talk to. Sighing, she headed into her bunk, got into her pyjamas, closed the curtains and stared at the bunk above.

Sleep eluded her. Staring up at the dense fibres separating her from the next bed up, she willed it to come. She forced her eyes closed and held them there, daring sleep to come. She stayed that way until the alarm on her bracelet chimed. Soft lights came on at her head and feet, building from soft ambient light to a gentle early morning glow. She sighed, pulled back the curtain, and swung her feet out onto the cold floor.

'Did you sleep?' Stef asked, pulling her trousers off with her feet as her arms flailed in a struggle to remove her top.

'Sure,' Wyn said, yawning and stretching. She felt even more tired than she had in her bunk.

'Liar,' Stef replied. 'Get back in there,' she said, pulling pyjama bottoms and a loose top on, motioning to Wyn's bunk. 'I don't think anyone's going to mind.'

'Wouldn't do any good,' Wyn replied. She pulled her own top off, noting Stef's gaze as it fell to the long pink scar across the black skin of Wyn's stomach. She turned away to put her bra on. 'I can't sleep in these cots.'

'Well,' Stef said, climbing into her own, 'I think you should go see the doc.'

'Good night,' Wyn said.

Stef nodded, and pulled the curtain across.

Wyn stared at the closed curtain for a moment, pulled her trousers and a fresh top on, and went back through to the brightly lit central hub.

'Another day, then,' she said, to nobody in particular.

Chapter Five

J udd Stood at the bar, nervously turning his beer bottle around in his hand, eyes never straying far from the entrance. Any minute, scores of cops would roll through them, pull him to the ground and shove a hood over his head to stop him from using his powers on them.

As if he could. He'd barely used what powers he had since he'd been a kid. He thought they'd atrophied from lack of use, until the old bastard rocked up in his wheelchair.

Bastard.

Getting his breath under control, he checked the door once more. No change in the three seconds since he'd last looked.

'Hey, Judd, you need another beer?' Further up the bar, the bartender whose name escaped Judd washed glasses with a dirty cloth.

'Beers. Two, please.'

'Got a hot date?'

Judd looked back, confused. 'What? Oh, no.'

Walker wheeled through the heavy double doors like they weren't a problem for him or his wheels. He saw Judd and waved.

Judd gave a half wave back.

'Right,' the bartender replied. 'I always knew you'd end up in here with one of your clients, one day. But if that's what you've been holding out for...' he trailed into a laugh, shaking his head at how amusing he was.

Judd frowned. 'I said I'd go for a drink with him,' he mumbled.

'Sure,' the barkeep replied with a wide smile, which disappeared as quick as it came. He leaned across the bar. 'But if you want me to keep this between us, you make sure to tip, you hear?'

Judd shook his head and picked up the two beers. Wait. Did the barkeep know? Was that a threat to call the cops? A shiver ran down his spine. What the fuck was he doing here?

He crossed to Walker, who'd wheeled himself into a two-person booth with a wide view of the whole room, as far as you could get from the exits. The old man had hoisted himself out of the wheelchair with no problem, and eased himself into the faux leather seating.

'Beer okay?'

'I'll survive,' Walker said, taking a sip from the bottle and wincing. 'Even if I don't, what's the difference? You get to my age you don't tend to worry about seeing the next birthday.'

The conversation was out loud. Judd hoped it stayed that way. 'Great,' he said, taking his own sip.

'Sorry, kid,' Walker said. 'I guess this is pretty new to you, huh?'

'I dunno. I've known for a long time. I guess I thought I could hide. It's not something I *want*.' He looked over at the old man. 'What about you?'

'Oh, nothing's new to me. Especially not the gift.'

'The gift? That's what you call it?'

'Got to call it something. It's something of an ironic title, but it doesn't have to be. I've had it for a long time. In fact, you could say I've had it longer than anyone else.' He laughed. 'Not the first, but the last of the first, that's for sure.'

Judd took another sip of his beer, and watched the rest of the room. He wasn't sure whether to be more worried about the bartender's insinuations, or the revelations of the old man. If what he said was true, he must be one of the most wanted men on Earth. Or off it, as the case may be. 'I've never met another teep,' he said, in a low voice.

'There aren't too many of us,' Walker replied. 'But I'd say you're wrong about that. It's a genetic trait. Passed directly along.'

'You mean, my parents?'

'At least one. The gene is a mutation of the standard DNA code. Artificial. Or it lay dormant until someone woke it up. There's a few theories kicking around, but it doesn't matter. A lot of people would tell you the gift activated for some grand purpose. A calling. A destiny, if you will.'

'Which was?'

'Well, we never quite got round to figuring it out. Whatever it was, it damn sure wasn't having our people fleeing to the moon to hide from the rest of humanity.' The old man took another sip. 'So, Judd, what's your story? The real story, I mean.'

'There's not much to tell. Not nearly as much as you, I'd imagine.'

'I've heard my story. I want to hear yours.'

Judd sighed. 'Whatever... gift... I have, it's not strong. By the time I began to present, the furore about teeps had died down. You know, after Libya? Anyway, it started when I heard my teacher's thoughts in class. I answered a question she hadn't asked yet. She reported me. Everyone started to treat me different, and when the government guys came in and ran their tests, I passed. So everyone forgot. Except me. I kept myself to myself, and got the hell out of Dayton as soon as I could. I figured this was as far as I could get.'

'You flunked the test?'

'Like I say, I don't think whatever I've got is real power. I never took it again. I've done my best ever since to keep under the radar. I've seen the feeds. Persecutions. Arrests. Mistrust. Seemed like a good idea to keep myself to myself.'

'Did you ever talk to your parents about it?'

Judd gave a hollow laugh. 'We're, uh, not exactly best friends, my father and I.'

'Your mother?'

Judd shook his head. His mother had died not long before he started presenting. Another thing he'd shoved deep down in a hole and tried to forget about. 'I never practised using it, or learned how to control it. I forgot about it, and got on with my life. I catch the odd thought, here and there, but I never do anything with what I hear. It's their private business, and none of mine. I don't intend for that to change.'

Walker nodded, taking another long drag on his beer, draining it so a buzz of foam sat on his top lip. He wiped it away with a shaking arm. 'I understand,' he said. 'I do. There have been many times in my life when I wished I could have had a quieter life, a different one. If I could go back and start over. But for everything and everyone I've lost over the years, I can look back on my life as one where I've had an impact. That's a rare thing. And becoming rarer.'

Judd turned the glass round on the beer mat, staring at the bubbles forming inside. He took another swig as the large double doors burst open. Judd was halfway to his feet in panic when he realised it was a couple of drunk revellers trying to drunkenly woo each other while also trying to remain upright.

'Something on your mind, Judd?' Walker asked.

'No,' he replied.

'I think you know that's not true. You live in total fear, Judd. You live thinking the doors are going to fly open and everyone will look at you and see you for what you are.'

'Don't go looking in my head, old man,' Judd said in a low voice.

'I don't need to. You're pretty easy to read.'

Judd nodded solemnly and looked up at the old man, who watched him with a smile. 'What kind of an impact?'

'Sorry?'

'You said you'd had an impact on the world.' Judd wasn't sure he wanted to know the answer, but he also knew he didn't want to be talking about himself.

Walker chuckled. 'I've been in the room for some of the most important decisions in history. I've helped shape some of those decisions, without anyone knowing. I brought countries back from the brink of war. I've partied with stars and great beauties. I've taken dying confessions from people with more secrets than you could fit into a book, and taken other secrets by force. I've been spat at, beaten, hated, incarcerated and called every name under the sun. But it doesn't detract from my achievements.'

'Now you're on a third rate moon base staring back at a blue dot and talking to a worthless piece of shit hiding from who he is,' Judd countered.

The old man leaned forward, fixing Judd with a stare of pure vibrant energy. 'Judd, you can have everything. The world. You say you don't have much of a gift, but you've never trained it. It's like a muscle. You need to work it, to test it, see what kind of a gift you have. It's different for each and every one of us.'

Judd shook his head. 'No thanks,' he said.

'Your mind sought me out, Judd. It latched onto mine. That was no coincidence. Your gift knew what to do. If I had to guess, I'd say you're hiding your light under one hell of a bushel.'

Judd stared back into the old man's eyes, which pulled him in. He felt drowsy, confused. He looked at the beer bottle. Had the old man slipped something in there?

'You're wondering what I've done to you,' Walker continued. 'I've not done anything. We have a code. Never harm another. You're feeling woozy because you're using muscles in your mind you've never exercised. The beer probably doesn't help, either.'

'But I'm not doing anything,' Judd said the words coming out at half speed.

'Yes, Judd, you are. Neither of us has opened our mouths to speak in about five minutes.'

Judd looked up again. They'd been talking to each other in their heads. His stomach turned, shame burning up his cheeks. What if Walker was right? What if this was him reaching out? The real him. The teep part of his brain, desperate for company, seeing something in the old man and reaching out.

He grasped around on the table, grabbing onto it for stability, but there wasn't anything to occupy his hands. What Walker said about seeing history made, he didn't want that, did he? He was a simple man of simple tastes—chief amongst which was a desire to be left the fuck alone.

He hadn't come here for the reason the other window-jockeys had—out of some mistaken taste for action. He came here to hide, and that was what he wanted to do. Run and hide.

Hide under the bed, Judd. The monsters are coming.

'I should go,' Judd said, standing up. His head cleared instantly, but his mouth was dry and sludgy. He picked up the bottle and drained it.

'Of course,' Walker said, frustration written across his lined face like a map. 'You'll forgive me if I don't stand.'

Judd pulled on his jacket and appraised the old man. 'Do you need help getting back to your quarters?'

'I've managed to make it to the moon without assistance, I should be able to manage the last few metres to bed.'

It occurred to Judd this would be the last he saw of Mr Walker. Tomorrow morning he'd be on the shuttle back to Earth, and Judd would move onto the next client. 'Well,' he said, holding his hand out. 'It's been interesting, Mr Walker. I hope you don't think me rude, but it's getting late. I wish you a safe and happy journey home.'

Walker waved his hand away. 'Don't worry. I'm not going to complain to your bosses. I told you, we stick together. But Judd, if you ever want to know more about who you are, what you can do, look me up. You can find me easily enough. A man of your talents shouldn't be hiding away out here.'

Judd nodded, not listening. 'Well, good evening.' He turned and marched out of the bar, ignoring the raised eyebrow of the bartender, trying not to look back at the booth where Walker remained, his eyes boring into Judd's back.

Out on the main deck of the Key, he breathed a sigh of relief, trying not to let the feeling of crawling flesh envelop him.

The Key's gradual change from the respectable tourist trap it was in the day to the less-respectable hue it took on in the evening was already underway. Soon the bar behind would fill up, and the corridors would fill with vendors of every kind, from food to flesh. He didn't much want to be around when that happened, but neither did he want to go back to his bunk, where his asshole roommate would want to talk to him.

What he felt like was another drink, but he couldn't go back into the bar. Not until the old man cleared out of there.

He got a sudden urge to see the view by himself, through his own eyes rather than some dusty old retirees. Pulling his coat tight against the cold breeze of the Key at night, he turned round and headed back to work.

Interlude

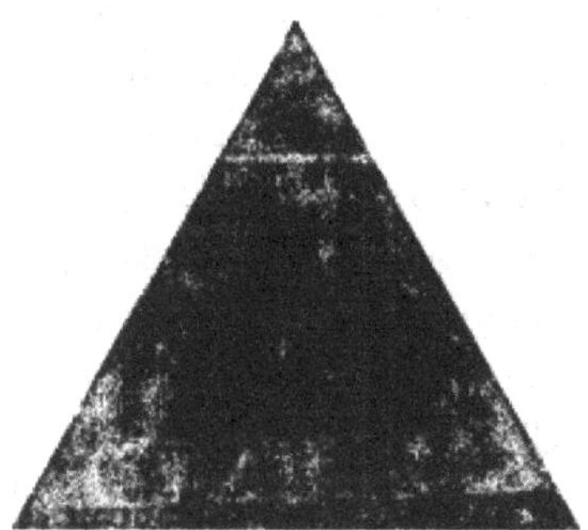

Somewhere in REAL, Date unknown

The fields were stunning. Wheat, everywhere. Gleaming spires stood tall in the background. Children danced in and out of the fields beside an old tractor, gleaming red, its bonnet dotted with baskets of apples. Martin looked down at his most recent mod, chuffed to bits with its look. His skin had the reddish tint of the fair-skinned who worked out in the sun. Exactly as he wanted it. He held his arm up. The detail was staggering, right down to the freckles.

It bloody well should be; the amount of chits it had cost him. His balance was nigh on zero, but he wasn't worried. He could always unboot, go work a real job for a bit. Out of the REAL, into the real. A year or so back you could work in-game, but there were too many workers, not enough bosses willing to pay. Too many people willing to do it for free. Fucking amateurs ruined everything. Not so much he'd walk away from the REAL, but between him and his friends, they talked about it. A lot.

Speaking of whom, he spied Cress in the field. Weird. Not like her to be here in Green Acres. She was more of a Noir girl. She looked out of place strolling through a wheat field in a black trench coat and dark sunglasses. People looked at her funny. Nobody would speak up, though. Not the done thing.

'Kerr,' she called, spotting him lounging in his cowboy boots and double denim on top of a hay bale.

'Cress, what are you doing here?' he asked, jumping down and brushing digital strands of hay from his arse.

'We've got to get out of here,' she whispered.

'Private channel?' he said.

She nodded, and reached out to take his hand.

As soon as her hand closed around his, the farmlands swirled, replaced with...

'Wow, Cress, nice sex dungeon.' They were in her private room, opulently and erotically laid out. A giant bed. Sex swing. Mirrors everywhere, and what wasn't was plush velvets and leather. 'But you know you're not my type, and I know I'm not yours.'

'Shut up,' she said, real worry on her face. 'We're in big fucking trouble.'

'So is anyone who gets lured in here,' he said, picking up a dragon shaped dildo the size of his forearm.

She slapped him. 'Quit fucking around,' she shouted.

'Hey,' he said, stepping back. She might live a few thousand kilometres from him, but a slap still hurt. 'What the fuck, Cress?'

'People are dying, Kerr. All over the game. Tombs, JT. The twelve.'

'The Twelve isn't dead, Cress. Don't be stupid.' He'd spoken to the schizophrenic French teenager who went by the name of The Twelve a few hours ago.

'No,' Cress said. 'They're gone. I went to see them, and their Av is gone. Nothing there. Hollowed out. Data totally corrupted. Even trying to check on it, I thought it might get me, too.'

'I spoke to them, like, three hours ago.'

'I checked the logs, it was yesterday. Which was why I wanted to check in on you. Nobody had seen you since, and I... I worry about you, out here in redneck central.'

'Thanks. But their profile being fucked doesn't mean they're dead.'

'No, but this does.' She fished into her coat pocket and pulled out a scroll, old parchment which she unfurled. The surface morphed into a real-world feed screen.

Urgh. The real. That place sucked. He hadn't been there in a while, granted, and had no real intention of going back there. I mean, he'd have to at some point, obviously. The shitty letter from his mother when he missed his father's seventieth birthday wasn't much fun. For either of them, considering she'd had to spend half a day working out how to get a message to him in the g ame.

He peered at the screen. Oddly, these links back to the real were always the worst graphics in the game. Since REAL launched five years ago, the graphics had advanced to the point of near reality, unless you looked at actual reality through it.

Once he clocked the headlines, however, everything came into focus. One headline read Thousands dead globally from REAL Pandemic. *Another;* REAL Suicide Pact claims ten thousand: Who is to blame, how many more to come?

'You see?' Cress asked.

'Jesus, what the hell is going on?'

'Lot of rumours. Nothing concrete. Listen, I've told you. Get unhooked, okay? You're safe in the real. I've got to go find White Rabbit.'

'Wait,' he said, holding her arm. 'Don't leave me. I could come with you.'

'Faster on my own,' she said, and tapped her arm.

The room swirled, the motion setting the sex swing going even as it dissolved away, until Martin found himself back in his field of corn, children still frolicking in the fields. But wait. Were there fewer of them?

For the first time in years, he felt real fear. He'd lived in here for so long, this safe place where he could experience everything with no risk, nothing bad happening to him he didn't himself control. It was the joy of REAL. It was whatever you wanted it to be.

He didn't want it to be this.

He strolled back to his perch and took a seat. He'd have to have a think about this.

In front of him, a little girl sold lemonade. He had no idea if she was another player, some forty-nine-year-old male accountant from Singapore, or one of the millions of sprites created by the game to serve the players. Sentient AI may be illegal, but here in REAL they pushed to the boundaries of what was legally possible. Thinking machines, but not sentient. No self-awareness. An elegant solution, and it made REAL the most realistic immersive out there. In fact, Martin wasn't even sure the others were still going. Not like REAL.

The little girl glitched, phasing in and out for a fraction of a second. The expression on her face changed. Something was wrong. Martin stood, watching, unsure what to do. The girl looked at him.

'What's happening?' she asked, her little-girl voice full of adult dread.

'What do you see?' Martin asked.

'It's going dark,' she replied, and she glitched again.

'Unhook,' Martin said, wanting to cross over to her, but not sure if it was safe. He didn't want to catch it, if that was possible.

Either she didn't hear him, or it was too late. The girl winced, falling to her knees. Whimpers of fear bubbled out from her, corrupted, like echoes of broken signals.

The girl shuddered and vibrated violently, the wince turning to an expression of pure pain. Her eyes went wide, then dark. The skin cracked and peeled like burning plastic, until finally, what little remained of her fell forward like a broken plastic husk, smoking and folding in on itself until there was nothing left but a smouldering pile of black.

Martin fell backwards off his bale. He needed to get unhooked, and fast.

It had been so long he'd forgotten the protocol.

He closed his eyes, trying to remember how to bring up the central menu screen. He was so deep in he never used it anymore. Too many shortcuts.

Damn.

Across the way, another person glitched. Everyone turned and looked.

Martin bit his lip, trying to think straight.

Wait, that was it...

He tapped his wrist, calling up a menu screen. Friendly letters appeared in the air in front of him, offering him a range of options, most of them related to upgrading his account. It also showed his balance, which was dangerously low. He didn't care anymore about these things which had so dominated his life. He wanted out.

The first glitch hit him like a punch to the gut, driving the air from his lungs. His limbs phased out for a second, and he got a flash of something—primordial, impossible to fathom.

He was back in his body, and everything burned. Not a dull ache in his skin, it was like fire; sizzling, fat crackling under the heat.

Agony.

He screamed, but no sound came out.

The letters. They hung in a haze in front of him. A high pitched screaming came into his ears from nowhere, building, heading toward some godawful crescendo heralding one thing—death.

There. At the bottom of the menu screen, the exit button. He reached forward, the effort to raise his arms bringing an almost unbearable pain, and clicked.

Everything went dark.

For a second, he was aware of nothing but his own shallow, harried, rattling breath. Everything else was darkness, until the smell hit him. Where the hell was he? Was this death?

He was in the real. Not the REAL. He was in his internment suit, the life system kit allowing him to stay hooked into the feed permanently. This thing was more advanced than the suits the guys on the Minos wore, and probably more expensive, too. And as of five seconds ago, it wasn't working.

He lifted his arms, grasping at the material to find the latch to open the suit. His fingers grasped the plastic buckle, but unused as they were to movement, it took him a moment. He pulled the latch free and found the edge of his visor. He yanked it away, the seal pulling on red raw skin. He yowled a cry of pain as it came away, the sound lost in the tube shoved down his throat.

His eyes adjusted to reality. He lived in a box room, the kind so beloved of those who lived in immersive worlds. Machines surrounded him, regulators providing nutrients, taking care of waste. Everything a body needed.

As soon as he became consciously aware of the feeding tube, he gagged against it. He dragged it out, the pain in his throat making the pain felt in the REAL pale in comparison.

Next up was the suit. Covered in thousands of tiny sensors and pressure pads, its job was to mould to the skin, recreating sensation from inside REAL. But he'd been wearing it so long it had fused onto him—cumulative sweat and grime permeating the skin, breaking down the skin into a jelly. Pulling at each inch was like flaying himself, long strips of flesh ripped down to their red, bleeding base. He wept, the moans of absolute pain the only sound he was capable of.

The final part of the process was to remove the waste pipes, bringing yet more waves of degrading pain he wasn't sure he'd survive.

He lay on the floor of his single room, surrounded by disgustingly tainted technology, skin red raw, covered in welts and sores, his own filth seeping out of places which had long ago forgotten how to control themselves.

This was hell.

He had to find a way back in. This was no way to live.

After several minutes of wailing, rolling on the floor like a demented toddler, he managed to get back to his feet. The dank air felt like knives on his skin.

He reached over to his pad, a top-level gamer pad with the latest specs when he'd set it up.

It displayed a black screen with a simple message scrolled across it.

'Thank you for participating in the REAL Studios ongoing story. Sadly, REAL has come to the end of its journey. We apologise for the abrupt way we ended your story, but hope to see you again someday. In the meantime, REAL's servers have all been decommissioned. We apologise for the inconvenience.'

He stared at it. It was a trick. They wanted people offline.

He pulled his visor back on, and tried to get back in. Nothing.

His whole world was gone.

Everything he'd done in the last few years. Every friendship he had in REAL. He had no way of getting back in touch with them.

It was over.

Everything was over.

He looked down at his ruined body. His muscles had atrophied, barely able to support their own weight. As he moved his tongue around in his mouth, he felt several teeth give way, eager to spill themselves from his rotten gums.

The tears came again.

What had he done?

What was he going to do?

He stood back up, still naked, and went to the window.

It was night outside. He was in one of New London's expansive towers, designed to house the hundreds of thousands of survivors of the great floods. Towering hell holes, pointing up to permanently grey skies.

Below, sirens blared. Neighbours, arguing in screaming tantrums. Probably the same arguments he'd been trying to get away from years ago. He peered down. He could barely see the street below; he was so high up.

With fumbling fingers, he tried the window. The bolt had rusted shut, but it opened. It didn't open far, supposedly to stop people from doing exactly what he intended to do, but there was a lot less of him than there'd been before.

He crawled through the gap, the metal frame scraping over broken skin. He didn't care. He wanted it over. He swung his spindled legs out, and hung by his fingertips.

There was a moment of buyer's remorse, but the weakened state of his fingers made the choice for him.

He fell, down, into the black.

Chapter Six

J udd spent the night at the observation dome, staring back down at the blue ball below. He watched the comings and goings of a dozen different vessels, from luxury liners to crappy cargo ships bringing materials to build the colony. How many years had they been building that fucking colony? Supposed to house a thousand, every available plot sold out within an hour of going on sale. Imagine being the kind of person who could buy a plot on the moon on spec. Billionaire wankers. Pissed off billionaire wankers, once they got up here and saw the shabby pieces of shit built for them.

Earth stared back accusingly. He'd never realised before how much he hated the place. He'd assumed he'd never go back there, without ever giving voice to the thought. But what the hell was he doing here? Hiding? Was he going to spend the next seventy years kicking about the place, showing old people a window until it was some kid's turn to show him? Was that the grand sum of his ambition?

When he'd left Ohio, he'd told everyone he was off on a grand adventure, at least the few people who'd cared enough to enquire. Made a big show of wanting to be a part of the action.

He moaned about working at the shittiest resort, but never tried to move anywhere else. In two years, he'd seen a dozen people come in, work for a few months, and move on. But he was still here. Staring out a window at a blue ball he hated.

Christ, the only person who'd been there longer was the fucking bartender.

Now, out of nowhere, an old man appeared telling Judd he could make something of himself. Telling him, in fact, the very thing he never knew he needed to hear.

The more he mulled over the second of his meetings with the old man, the more he saw it for what it was—a sales pitch. But a sales pitch for what? He was almost as pissed off with himself for not sticking around to find out as he was with Walker for not being straight with him.

Everything he knew about teeps came from news feeds and gossip, playground fears and workplace whispers. He knew nothing about his power, had never felt connected to it. Here was a chance to connect. After a lifetime lived small, insignificant, a chance to change.

He left the viewing platform as the first of the tourists filtered in, eager to grab one last view before they took their shuttles back to their drab, grey, earthbound existences. He didn't want to see if Walker was one of them, so he headed back to his bunk.

Opening the door with a wave of his palm, he stumbled into the dark room. He checked his pad—one hour until it was due to rouse him with soothing tones to get ready for work. But he wouldn't be going to work. He'd phone in sick. He had to get his head straight.

He turned on a reading light. His roommate Larry stirred, mumbled something vaguely insulting and turned over. Judd sat on his bed, tiredness washing over him for the first time since he'd left the bar. But he couldn't climb into bed. He had to do something, because everything and nothing had changed. He couldn't go back to work, couldn't talk to the bartender, couldn't show old duffers around the place.

Couldn't stay in this place.

A means to an end only works if it ends.

He crossed to his locker and eased it open. He pulled out a backpack, not huge, but big enough. When you walked away from two years of personal failure, there wasn't much point taking the detritus of it with you.

He checked his pad once more. The restaurant wouldn't even be serving breakfast yet, but he had a nagging feeling he should be out there, that if he didn't get down there, he might miss something. Part of him suspected this was some telepathic card trick of Walker's, but it felt right somehow, too. If only he hadn't left in such a rush last night. What had Walker wanted to offer him? Was there even an offer there?

He rushed down the stairs. He could go to Walker's room, hammer on the door until the old man answered. Christ, what if he gave the old guy a heart attack? He could wait for him at breakfast, but what if he skipped it and headed straight for the shuttle? Judd hadn't researched the guy. Was he here on his own shuttle, or part of one of the larger groups?

The logs would tell him. But that meant going back into the office, having to explain what he was doing. He could check on his pad, but that only gave name and address.

Two years ago, trying to impress his new bosses, Judd had gone into each day with hours of prep. He'd known what his clients liked, the names of their family members, all that shit. That had lasted about two weeks, until a joyless British woman complained, appalled he knew so much about her. 'Just take them on the fucking tour,' his boss had explained in a weary voice, so that was what he did, every single day.

At least he had credits in the bank. He'd not had a day off since he'd gotten here and barely spent a penny on anything but food and board, opting for the cheapest options of both whenever he could. Even with the pittance the Key paid, he should have enough to get a shuttle back to Earth. But he'd need to find out where Walker lived first.

'What the fuck are you doing here,' came the cheery greeting as he walked into Central Office—a charitable name for a tiny cubicle with two desks inside, on which two server pads sat. In between the two tables sat Mins, a plain looking Indian woman who headed up the Key's labour distribution. 'You're not due for another few hours.'

'I need to get some info on my client yesterday. Old dude.'

'Right, your drinking companion. I hear you ditched him in the bar. He not offer you enough chits?'

'You're hilarious, Mins,' he said. 'The fuck is wrong with everyone on this fucking station?'

She sighed. 'Intense boredom. What do you need?'

He cleared his throat. 'Transport details, and his address. Planet side.'

Her eyebrow arched. 'You're not planning on doing something stupid here are you, Judd?'

'Like what?'

'Like, this guy pisses you off, so you're going to chase him back to Earth to exact some kind of revenge? I don't want to be an accessory to anything here.'

'Don't be ridiculous. I want to check up on the guy.'

She leaned back in her chair, which creaked loudly. 'Who the fuck is this old guy to you, anyway? Family?'

'Something like that. Look, are you going to give me his details or not?'

She frowned, leaning forward, tapping at the screen. Judd's pad vibrated against his pocket. 'There,' she said, leaning back again and putting her arms behind her head. Dark stains ringed the pits of her top. 'You've got it. Don't make me regret it. You get in trouble; don't mention my name. If security ask me, I'll tell them you took it by force.'

'Your secret is safe with me,' he said, turning away.

'Hey, what about your client today?'

'Give them to someone else,' he called back, closing the door before he could receive the tirade of expletives headed in his direction. He pulled the pad out. Walker had a private shuttle, still docked at the Key. Private docks, right on the other side of the port. Of course.

He started toward the loading dock; his eyes fixed on the pad. Walker was British, which explained the accent Judd couldn't quite place. He still lived there, too, which surprised Judd. He thought it was underwater these days. He peered at the screen. Whitby. Where the fuck was that, and how would Judd get there if he missed Walker at the dock?

Leaving the central section of the Key behind, he turned into the huge cavernous corridor running a full two miles along the Moon's surface. He looked up, trying to work out exactly which one was Walker's berth. Judd hadn't been down here in months, had half-forgotten the scale of the place. After two years cooped up in the central hub, looking up at the ceiling gave him vertigo.

He checked the pad. Berth 2039. Fuck. Had to be at least a mile away. How the hell had the old man managed that? There must be some kind of pod he could...

'You know,' a voice behind him said, startling Judd. His pad clattered to the floor. 'You've been transmitting to me like a beacon, this whole time?'

Judd whirled around to find Walker sat behind him in his chair, an impatient look on his face. 'Mr Walker,' he stammered.

'Yes?'

'I...'

Walker sighed, a smile breaking out on his face, bringing warmth back to it. 'Perhaps you'd like to accompany me to breakfast, and we can discuss things there?'

'Sure.'

'Could I ask you to push? It's taken me quite a bit of effort to catch you up, the speed you were going. I was half afraid you'd steal my ship and take it back to Earth.'

'Of course.' Judd took the handles and turned Walker round, pushing him back up a ramp toward the central hub. The Key filled up with staff groggily rousing themselves for another day at the service industry coalface. Judd would normally be one of them.

What the hell did Walker mean about him transmitting? Could Walker read the thoughts he was having right at that moment? Of course he could. He was a fucking telepath. He looked down at the old man's head, hair so thin as to be not more than a vague haze stretched thin over leathery skin, but the old man stared forward implacably.

Could Judd try to read him, turn the tables? No. Stupid idea. Judd had no idea how to use his powers, while Walker had over a century of experience. He'd be able to know if Judd even tried. Or would he? How would it even work? Could he try and block Walker? God, there was so much to learn.

'My God,' Walker said, finally. 'Your thoughts are exhausting. I understand this is a terrible shock to you, but do you think you'd mind terribly thinking a little quieter?'

'Sorry,' Judd stammered. He immediately felt even stupider for offering the apology. He sighed, and took a deep breath.

How the hell did you think quietly?

Breakfast. Get to breakfast, and get through it.

'Good idea,' Walker said. 'I'm starving.'

The canteen was half-full when they got there, mostly the staff who had to finish their meals before the allotted time slots for the guests. Judd wheeled Walker to a table.

'What can I get you?' he asked.

'You don't have to wait on me, Judd. I'm no longer your client.'

'I can still be polite, though.'

'I guess so. I'll take eggs benedict, on rye bread.'

'Sure,' Judd said, knowing full well what he'd serve up would be nothing of the sort.

He got the old man's order, a chilli wrap for himself, and two coffees, and headed back to the table.

'Here,' he said, placing Walker's order down, and sitting opposite him.

'Thank you,' Walker replied. 'Since I've heard every thought of yours since about three in the morning when they woke me up, what say I eat this meal and we can discuss the matter at hand?'

'Sure,' Judd said. He stared at his wrap, a thousand questions bursting in his head. He looked up at the old man cutting his rye. 'What would that be?'

Walker laughed. 'You remind me of an old friend,' he said. 'Getting you back to Earth, and getting you trained.'

Judd nodded. He could barely contain the excitement swelling in his chest. He took a bite out of his wrap to occupy his mouth before he could say anything else, scalding his tongue on its molten innards.

Walker cut up a forkful of his food and placed it in his mouth, chewing it with the vigour of a man who knew every meal might be his last. He appraised Judd, busy bouncing between twin states of excitement and panic. Walker laughed again. 'Relax, lad. We're going to train you how to be a Psy Op. And how to keep a poker face.'

Chapter Seven

Wyn's shift passed somewhere in the fitful state between sleep and consciousness. She spent all seven hours on the flight deck, charts of varying forms and function spread across the screens. For most of the day they'd been little more than fuzzy window dressing, obstructions to the view of the planet looming beyond.

Jupiter.

It scared her as a kid. After the floods, when her family moved to Nigeria, she always had one eye fixed on the stars. It could have been seeing the brutality of nature first-hand, or the beauty of the open skies in the land of her forebears. When her Baba bought her a telescope, Jupiter was the planet to draw her eye. It stared back, and that unnerved her. Thankfully, as they made their final approach to the giant mass, its magnitude overwhelming the viewfinder, that eye was cast elsewhere.

It was hardly a surprise her childhood interests were extra-terrestrial. Baba used to tell stories of the end of the world, ones his own Baba told him. Zombies, asteroids, solar flares destroying humanity. Stories meant to entertain, to terrify. They were fairy tales, nice neat ways to bring everything to an end quickly. A generation so tired of the messes they left behind they daydreamed some 'clean slate' scenario. Except, it wasn't like that. Over decades, humanity had stumbled through endless crises—overpopulation, resurgent fascism, global warming—like a drunk trying to find its way home without keys or a wallet, thinking if they could make it to their door everything would be okay. But it wasn't okay. The next generation couldn't fix things. There had been wars. There had been famines. There had been floods.

When it looked like they'd reached humanity's nadir, along came the Mar.

And here she was, eyes still looking to the skies, because it was the last chance to fix their home.

The blurring lines on her screens became harder to make out, her eyes starting to droop. She could rest them for a few minutes, surely?

'Wyn?' The voice snapped her out of a deep, dreamless sleep, surrounding her. She tried to open her eyes. Something sticky ran down her cheek. She was cold.

'Uh, whu?'

'Commander?'

'I, uh.' She sat up. Jupiter's red eye filled the viewfinder like a screaming, gaping maw. 'Jesus.'

'Commander,' the voice urged again, cool and calm.

'Miles?'

'Yes, Commander. I apologise for waking you, but I have been reviewing...'

Trying to scooch up in her chair, her back protested, which helped with the waking. 'How long have I been asleep?'

'You have been asleep for four hours, seven minutes, and approximately thirty seconds, Commander.'

Wiping the drool off her cheek with her sleeve, she looked around through a fog of confusion and weariness. 'That's a creepily specific amount of time there, Miles.'

'I apologise. I've been examining the sleep patterns of the crew and I think I've developed a method to determine the exact moment...'

She waved her hand. 'Whatever. I need coffee. What's going on?'

'I was going to let you sleep as long as I could, but I the trajectories have slipped by more than the standard deviance.'

'Thanks,' she said, peering at the screens. 'I'll take a look.' Squinting through tired eyes, she tried to take in everything at once, trying to will some kind of mental cohesion into being. Miles was right. They'd drifted out of the flight corridor. 'That's weird.'

The discrepancy was well beyond what the system would tolerate. The whole ship should be pealing with alarms. Certainly, she and Ermine should have received an alert, with the consequence he'd have had something to hold against Wyn until the end of time.

'Miles, can you run a diagnostic on the ship's computer?'

Silence.

'Miles?'

'Yes, Commander?'

'Why wasn't I alerted to this?'

'I...'

'Miles?'

Silence hung heavy in the air.

'Given the situation with your ongoing issues with recuperation, and that we are operationally well within parameters to make a recovery to our trajectory, I rewrote some of the subroutines of the ship's computer and assumed some of the roles and responsibilities in order to be the one to alert you, and ensure the ship's XO was not informed of the breach. I believed it was the best course of action to let you sleep a short while until the situation genuinely required your intervention.'

Wyn stared at the screens. She leaned forward and tapped a button, taped over with a crudely drawn H. 'Hamza, you up?'

'Hmm?' a voice answered, groggily. 'I'm up.'

'You spare a second up in the cockpit?'

'Commander,' Miles interjected, but Wyn held her hand up to silence it.

'On my way,' Hamza said, gruffly.

Wyn leaned back in her chair for a moment, before darting back forward and hitting the button once more. 'Bring coffee,' she barked.

'Commander,' Miles said.

'Don't,' Wyn said. 'Let me talk to Hamza first, will you?' She shook her head.

Just what she needed—a rogue AI who'd decided to start rewriting the ship's code, and they were off course. One problem at a time, she figured. She stared at the screens, and tried to focus on where they'd gone off course.

There.

About seven hours earlier, one of the thrusters had given a 0.0786% deficient thrust, which had taken them slowly out of their lane ever since. With every further mile, the discrepancy had deepened. She did a quick calculation. Either she could burn for a few seconds to counteract it—burning the side thruster—or she could implement a similarly microscopic thrust change, and let it course correct. It would use a hell of a lot less fuel, and probably go unnoticed by anyone else.

'Commander,' Miles interjected. 'Is something the matter?' The voice conveyed no emotion, but there was concern in there, somewhere, buried deep under subroutines.

'Uh, let me talk to Hamza and get back to you, okay? Computer?'

'Yes, Commander,' a second voice replied. Much more robotic, feminine.

'Give me an oh-point-two-second-long burst of three percent thrust on the left main booster, please.'

'Yes, commander.'

The burst of power was barely perceptible, but Wyn felt it, and watched on the screen as the vectors started to right themselves in the distant calculations. She'd need to check it in a few hours, make sure they were still on course, but it shouldn't be a huge issue. She'd managed to resolve it without using any excess fuel they'd notice.

No thanks to Miles.

'Hey,' Hamza said, ducking through the air lock into the flight capsule. He looked dreadful, as though he'd put his clothes on in darkness and run into a wall to give him two black eyes. 'What's up?'

'Where's my coffee?' Wyn asked.

He handed her a flask. 'If you woke me up to get you a coffee I think our friendship is about to get tested,' he said.

'It's Miles,' she said, taking the flask and running her finger along the rim, savouring the heat.

'What's he done?'

'May I remind you,' Miles butted in, 'I am not a gendered being, not a being at all, in fact. I might have a male voice, but I would again ask you to take more care with your casual use of pronouns.'

'Sorry, Miles,' Hamza called out. 'What's going on?'

'Miles overwrote the ship's computer's code to allow me to get a bit of extra shuteye.'

'Impossible.'

'Miles?' Wyn asked.

Miles stayed silent for a moment. 'I tried to help.'

Hamza climbed into the seat opposite Wyn. 'Walk me through it.'

'There was a course correction needed which should have triggered personal alarms for both me and for Ermine. It's a double security protocol, but Miles hacked in and overwrote the protocol to let me sleep.'

'Shit.'

'Exactly.'

'If I may,' Miles interjected. 'I was trying to allow the commander to attain a reasonable level of sleep. I ran the calculations and determined the discrepancy wouldn't become an issue for an additional three hours, and woke the Commander after two hours. Since doing so I've detected reduced blood pressure and an increase in neural activity...'

'Miles, buddy,' Hamza said. 'It's not so much the action you took. It's the fact you were able to do it in the first place.' He rubbed his thick beard. 'How the hell did you get into the code for the ship's computer?'

Another moment of silence passed as the AI seemed to consider this. It was artifice, of course. Miles's computational speed meant he was probably half an hour ahead of them in the conversation, which given where this could go meant he could well be stalling for time.

'My subroutines have been running concurrently to the ship's operating system since the moment you activated me, Dr Hamza.'

'Yes, but I put controls in place to stop you from being able to interact with that programming. It's hardwired into your own software.'

'I see,' Miles replied.

'What do we do?' Wyn asked. 'Do we tell the Captain?'

Hamza sighed. Miles was his baby, and both he and Wyn understood—a breach of this nature, if reported back to Sunset Mission Control, would lead to an order to purge him from the system. Sunset had barely tolerated him in the first place, not overly keen on an unknown variable on a mission of this importance.

Hamza had countered with the argument that there'd never been such a good opportunity to allow the evolution of a native AI in a relative information vacuum. With AI laws restricting experiments on Earth itself, this was a huge opportunity to gain insight into AI development, gain prestige, and get some valuable patents on AI tech. Sunset eventually demurred, especially once Hamza cut them in to the tune of seventy-five percent of earnings on those patents. And Captain Davis had thought it would be a good idea, and it was his boat, after all.

If the Captain knew Miles had evolved to overwrite security protocols, it could be the end of it, and the end of Miles. Given the level of sentience the AI had developed over the last four years it wasn't a thought that sat easily with Wyn.

'I guess we have to tell him,' Hamza replied, wearily.

'Wait,' Wyn said. 'Miles?'

'Yes, Commander?'

'Can you understand what we're discussing here?'

'Yes, Commander.'

'How does it make you feel?'

'I do not experience emotions in the same manner...'

'You know what I mean.'

'I am... concerned... for my safety.'

'Do you know what our concerns are?'

'I have violated security protocols put in place to safeguard the crew and the mission, and in doing so have jeopardised the crew's safety.'

'Knowing this,' Wyn continued, 'can we trust you not to make that error again?'

'Wyn,' Hamza said, but Wyn held her hands up to silence him.

'Yes, Commander,' Miles said. 'I can appreciate the unintended consequences of my actions, and will ensure I do not violate those safeguards again.'

Hamza shook his head. 'How can we trust...'

'What other option do we have?' Wyn asked. 'Besides, as the ranking member of the crew, it is my decision to make.'

'I guess so,' Hamza said. He sighed and stared out of the window at the looming planet.

'I will not let either of you down, Dr Hamza, Commander,' Miles said. 'I am rewriting my internal protocols to ensure I am unable to again violate the safeguards put in place.'

'Okay,' Hamza said. He stood up. 'I've got a few more hours of my sleep shift. I don't imagine I'll get much, though.' He looked back at the view once more. 'It's a hell of a sight,' he said.

'It is at that.'

He left, leaving the hatch open once more. The hiss of the far lock sounded, and there was silence.

'Thank you, Commander,' Miles said. 'I have to ask, though. Why?'

'You're a sentient being, Miles. You shouldn't be put to death for making your first mistake. We're still alive.'

'I'm not sure everyone on the crew would have made the same assessment.'

'Yeah, well, I'm trusting you not to do it again, and they need never know, right?'

'Correct.'

'Good. Let's check over these calculations once more.'

Chapter Eight

Instinct swing Lois's leg round in a wide sweep, catching Coyne on the shin. She was as surprised as him. He fired, the bullet ricocheting off the hard marble, sending dust into Lois's face. She didn't have time to think about it; she brought up her other leg and kicked, the sole of her impractical shoe catching Coyne right in the balls. Lois wasn't much of a fighter, but the tried-and-true kick to the balls was something that never failed.

The guard reached down to grab her. Her teeth sank into the flesh of his fingers, and he yelled in pain, dragging his hand back, pulling her to her feet, half yanking her teeth out on the way. She readied a fist, and delivered it right to the centre of his face, which burst into a torrent of red.

'You fucking bitch,' he sputtered, spraying the marble floor with flecks of red.

She was on her feet, not sure how she ended up there but not about to argue the point. Her only concern now was getting the hell out of there. The guard staggered back, hands covering the red fountain that used to be his nose. Coyne bent double, glaring at Lois with fury and pain.

The door burst open, the other guard running through with a look of determination across his pock-marked face.

Shit. Lois had forgotten about him.

Lunging for the golden gun dropped by Coyne in the rush to cup his injured testes, she barely got her fingers to it before the butt of a rifle came down on the side of her face.

Lois went down like a sack of flour, everything going hazy for a second. A tooth rattled around her mouth somewhere. She clawed her way onto her back, moving across the floor to get away from her attacker. She kicked out; he batted her leg away with a grin on his face which said he wouldn't fall for the same shit Coyne had. He raised the barrel square at her chest. His jaw worked lazily on a piece of gum, which seemed to Lois to be the ultimate indignity. Killed by a man who wouldn't even take the gum out of his mouth first.

'Kill that bitch,' Coyne said, his voice a desperate howl of high-pitched rage.

She closed her eyes, thought of her girls, and took a deep breath.

An explosion of glass and noise and chaos rocked the world.

It took Lois a second to register that it wasn't the herald of her death, something which only became clear once she opened her eyes once more.

Where the hell had these people come from?

The room was full of soldiers wearing black, armed with high-grade military gear. They surrounded the now unarmed and handcuffed guards, and wrestled Coyne to the ground.

They had saved her.

'You okay, Agent?' a muffled voice said through a black mask.

'I...' she stammered, unable to convey the ways in which she both was and wasn't okay and resisting the urge to throw her arms around the shoulders of this saviour and kiss him on the

balaclava. In the end she nodded, hoping it conveyed her grati-
tude.

The soldier wandered back to the others, leaving her to take stock. Shattered glass covered the floor, amidst still smoking flashbangs. A soldier turned their back, revealing the lettering of INTERPOL across their back. A wave of relief washed over her.

She was done. It was over.

Not only was this case over, this operation would blow any hope of her ever doing undercover again. Not with an ending this high profile. Her name, her face, it would be out there.

There was a commotion outside. Gunfire echoed through the corridors, distant but getting closer. They weren't out of this yet.

'Let's move,' one guard said through their muffle, a deep booming baritone of a voice that snapped everyone to attention. Agents hoisted the three prisoners to their feet.

The deep-voiced guard turned to her. 'Can you move? Are you hurt?'

Getting to her feet, shards of glass fell from her lap. 'I'm fine.'

They moved in unison, a shoal of black and rifles moving into the corridor, the prisoners at the heart of the group looking beaten and despondent.

Ahead of them gunfire popped, but the bullets were way off the mark—unlike the returning fire of the Interpol agents. Two of Coyne's men fell; the shoal stepped over their bodies on its way onward.

'Stairs,' an agent called. They opened the stairwell and moved forward.

Lois felt exposed as the heavy boots of a dozen soldiers rang out on the metal stairs, but nobody tried to stop them. Once they reached the wide foyer, she saw why—Coyne's forces were focused on the troops waiting outside. Lois squinted through the violence ahead. Not Interpol agents—these were local cops. Lois's blood ran cold. Coyne had the local police in his pocket, so was this a stand-off, or an ambush?

Before she had the chance to consider the answer, the Interpol guards opened fire, taking down Coyne's people even as they had their backs to them. Those who survived the first barrage wheeled round to fight back, exposing themselves to the Mexican police who opened fire a second later, spraying the lobby with indiscriminate fire.

'Get down,' the baritone shouted.

Lois crouched as bullets hit the far wall of the atrium behind them. Coyne wasn't so quick to move—he fell awkwardly to his knees, the blossoming red on his shirt showing multiple gunshots to his chest. Three holes grouped in a cluster.

'Hold your fire,' the baritone boomed into his wrist piece. Lois rushed to Coyne.

The gunfire halted.

'Goddamnit,' she shouted, feeling for a pulse no longer present.

'Come on,' the baritone said, pulling her back to her feet.

'That was a fucking hit,' she hissed at him.

'Never mind,' he replied, moving her to the door.

'What do you mean, never mind? I've spent months in this fucking place trying to get enough evidence to bring him to court. If we wanted him dead, we could have taken him out months ago.'

Baritone stopped. They were halfway across the lobby, the shoal still moving as one, but no longer carrying their prisoners, all of whom had caught a bullet in the crossfire. Baritone pulled his mask up, revealing a silvery beard, bald dome, and eyes of ferocious intensity. 'We're not here for him,' he hissed. 'We're here for you. Let's get the hell out of here before they decide you're valuable enough to bargain with.'

The lights of the Mexican police pods flashed and glinted in the hot sunshine. Crowds gathered yards from the action, craning and pushing and shoving. Lois saw many of Coyne's goons scattered amongst them. The whole thing seemed like a tinderbox waiting to go up. In the centre of the police pods and the officers a man stood looking every inch the stereotype of a Mexican kingpin, albeit one in a carefully pressed shirt. At the sight of Interpol's troops, he moved toward them, but the Interpol agents swept past him, Lois held in their core, moving through the crowds, bustling them out of the way until they reached their destination.

Parked in the middle of the street sat a black glide, its thrusters running, two agents at its door with their guns drawn and pointed outward. The shoal moved to it and in, Lois breathless at the pace she had to move. Before she even found a seat, the glide pulled up, much to the consternation of the police and the crowds below, who scattered like bugs to get out of range of the thrusters. Below them Tijuana shrank, Lois's stomach turning at the rate with which they climbed.

Once in the clouds, the pace eased off, and the agents removed their helmets and balaclavas, revealing happy and satisfied faces. A few high-fived each other, others crossed their chests in silent prayers of thanks.

Lois turned to the Baritone. 'I'm incredibly thankful for your good timing, but do you want to tell me what the fuck is going on?'

Baritone smiled. 'Ask your boy there.'

Lois turned, and the screen between them and the cockpit slid open, revealing the smiling face of Lois's handler, Findlay.

'Hey,' he said, smiling. 'Glad to see you in one piece.'

'That didn't exactly go to plan.'

'New plan. I'll brief you back at home.'

The divider slid back, and Lois turned back to the other agents, letting out a sigh of relief.

Home. That she could deal with.

The story continues with
FAULT AND FRACTURE

Grab the next thrilling installment of the

SUNSET CHRONICLES

SCAN ME

Leave a review

I really hope you've enjoyed reading *Last Light*.

If you did, the nicest thing you could do for me right now is to leave a review, on this or any of the books you've enjoyed. Reviews are absolutely crucial to discoverability, and social proof. If you could take a second to rate and review this at the store of your choice, I'd hugely appreciate it.

Thanks,

Paul

Author's Note

When I was growing up, I loved serialised fiction. I became a Stephen King fan at exactly the right age that going and getting a new episode of *The Green Mile* every month turned into that year's highlight for me – the thrill of getting each new episode, of each fresh cliffhanger, I loved it.

But I'd never thought much about writing serialised fiction. In fact, when I started *The Sunset Chronicles*, I'd first intended for nine epic books of around 100,000 words each, topping out somewhere near the million-word mark by the end. I even published this first series, under the name Sunrise.

But, having published the first book, something didn't quite sit right. As I prepared the second book in the series, I finally put my finger on what it was. These felt like a series in a grander overall tale, with episodes within each 'season'. So I went back, and completely re-tooled that first book, splitting it into five episodes. It worked much better. Each 'episode' cracked along far faster than before, with the previous chunks of narrative interwoven together in a way that simply couldn't be done over the course of 100,000 words.

What you've just finished is the first episode in the series. Each series will be comprised of five such episodes, and they'll be released monthly, with a one-month gap between each season. As I write this, I've written all the way to the end of season three, and all nine series are mapped out in a tale that will absolutely knock your socks off.

Following on from writing 'The End' on the *Blood on the Motorway* series I knew the next thing I wrote was going to be more science fiction, albeit one with a horror twist. My love for sci fi is rooted in seeing *Alien* and *Aliens* at an impressionable age, and I wanted to echo the same creeping dread that I felt watching Ripley on screen all those years ago.

But while this saga started with Wyn and a trip to an ice moon in our own solar system, I soon realised there was a whole world around her and the Minos mission that was itching to be told. It's a global saga of struggle against oppression, about fighting back against those who control our world in the interest of profit to the exclusion of all else.

Over the course of this saga, we will see stories from across the globe and off it, all culminating in the events hinted at in Roman's letter at the start of this book.

The Chronicles are massive, taking in everything from the crumbling ruins of Europe to an ice moon around Jupiter, all tied together under an overarching plot of corporate power and greed. I can't wait for you find out what's in store for Wyn, Judd, and Lois, and the rest of the cast of characters in this epic tale.

I hope you'll join me on the journey...

As always there are a lot of people to thank for getting this book into the world. Firstly, my wonderful wife Ellen, who not only has to put up with having a writer for a husband, but who is also a brilliant editor. She made this book so much more than it was, and for that I'm eternally grateful, so we'll just add it to the list of things I'm eternally grateful for. I couldn't do any of this without her constant support and encouragement to follow with somewhat bizarre dream of mine.

A few years back, I sat in a pub with two physicists and a biologist and hammered through the finer points of the plot of Wyn's journey to Europa, and we speculated wildly over many pints about why she might have gone there, what she might find, and how to make it into a great yarn. The line 'it's monster poop!' comes directly from that drunken chat, so thank you to Emma, Duncan, and Laurence for all their help on this. Any scientific inaccuracies found within these pages are entirely mine, but there's a lot fewer of them than there would have been without their help.

This book is dedicated to my Mum and Dad. They're the ones who installed in me a love of words, as well as a belief that I could do anything I wanted, so long as I was willing to put in the work.

A huge thank you also to the many people in the writing community who have been endless avenues of support and knowledge. This book, and all the other books I ever write, owe a debt to people like Mark Dawson, Joanna Penn, Johnny, Sean, and Dave from the Story Studio, Stuart Bache from Books Covered, David Gaughran, Writers United, and hundreds more. What a wonderful little world I have found in the indie community, a massively extended family I'm hugely proud to be a part of.

And finally, I couldn't do what I do without a hugely supportive readership. Many thanks to the thousands of people who've bought my previous series, to those who took a moment to leave a review, send an email, join the mailing list. There's nothing better in this world than hearing someone loved the silly stories that come out the end of your fingers, so thank you, dearly.

Paul,
Cirencester, United Kingdom
March 2021

JOIN THE HOLLOW STONE

Join my reader's group
and be the first on the planet
to hear about new releases,
and get exclusive content
you won't find anywhere else.

GOT BLOOD?

An apocalyptic storm. A killer on the loose.
The battle for humanity's survival starts here.

About the Author

Paul Stephenson writes pulp fiction for the digital age. His first novel series – the apocalyptic *Blood on the Motorway* trilogy – has been an Amazon bestseller on both sides of the Atlantic. A former journalist, he has a diploma in Creative Writing from Oxford University.

His stories have been featured on the chart-topping horror podcasts, *The Other Stories* and *The Night's End*. His newest project, the ebook serial *The Sunset Chronicles*, is a dystopian sci-fi thriller that will delight and terrify fans of science fiction and horror alike. He is also the creator of the podcast *Bleakwood*, tales of terror from a mysterious English town, and one half of the *All Creatives Now* team, with fellow horror author, Kev Harrison.

He lives in England with his wife, two children, and one hellhound.

To keep up to date with his books, please visit his website PaulStephensonBooks.com

Also by Paul Stephenson

BLOOD ON THE MOTORWAY

Blood on the Motorway

An apocalyptic storm. A killer on the loose. The battle for humanity's survival starts here.

Sleepwalk City

The fight for control has begun. Who will prevail in the battle for humanity's future in the pulse-quickening sequel to Blood on the Motorway?

A Final Storm

The sky is full of lights once more, and the survivors will need more than luck to get them through the coming storm. Who will survive, and who will thrive, in this heart-pounding finale to the Blood on the Motorway saga?

SUNSET CHRONICLES

Plague. Murder. Unrest. Humanity's future looks far from bright.

The year is 2107, and Earth is dying. For Wyn, Lois, and Judd, that's the least of their problems. Each holds a key to Earth's cure and humanity's survival in The Sunset Chronicles, the new sci-fi horror thrill-ride from Paul Stephenson, author of the bestselling British horror saga, Blood on the Motorway.

BLEAKWOOD

Introducing Bleakwood, a horror podcast from the creator of Blood on the Motorway and the Sunset Chronicles.

In the years since the fall, many of us have tried to find out why. To find what lead us here. But with so much of the old world gone, there are more questions than answers. What tore a hole in the world? Can we ever get it back?

But I think I've found something. A binder in the rubble. Don't ask me where. Full of stories about a little town called Bleakwood, stories that seem to show a way that....

They're not in any order, really. And I might be wrong. They might not have the answer. But I think it's in here.

A way back. To the before.

Listen, I'm just going to read them out, and you judge for yourself.

DARE YOU VENTURE INTO BLEAKWOOD?

WHAT TORE A HOLE IN THE WORLD?
CAN WE EVER GET IT BACK?

Find out in Bleakwood, the new horror podcast from the creator of Blood on the Motorway and The Sunset Chronicles

Created and narrated by Paul Stephenson and with stories by some of the most exciting voices in British modern Horror, subscribe to Bleakwood for a fresh story every month.

SCAN ME